IT'S FUN TO BE A
BRIDESMAID

ISBN 0-590-26592-X

Copyright © 1995 by Bluebird Toys (UK) Ltd. Under license from Origin Products Ltd.
All rights reserved. Published by Scholastic Inc.

Book designed by N.L. Kipnis

12 11 10 9 8 7 6 5 4 3 2 1   5 6 7 8 9/9 0/0

Printed in the U.S.A.   24

First Scholastic printing, April 1995

IT'S FUN TO BE A
BRIDESMAID

Written by CAROL THOMPSON
Illustrated by DARRYL GOODREAU

SCHOLASTIC INC.
New York   Toronto   London   Auckland   Sydney

One spring day James and Rebecca came to visit Polly. They had some important news to tell her.

"James and I are getting married," said Rebecca happily. "That's wonderful!" Polly exclaimed, giving each of them a hug and a kiss. "Congratulations!"

"But that's not all," James said mysteriously. "We want you to be in our wedding, Polly. How would you like to be a bridesmaid?"

"Oh!" cried Polly. "I'd love to!"

5

Soon Rebecca took Polly to the dressmaker to try on her bridesmaid gown. It was a little big. The dressmaker would have to alter the gown to make it fit. Polly stood very still while the dressmaker tucked and pinned the gown.

"That color looks lovely with your hair," Rebecca said.

Polly smiled. James was her favorite uncle, and Rebecca already seemed like an aunt.

At the wedding rehearsal, the director showed Polly how to walk in time with the music: right, together . . . left, together . . . right, together. It was hard to do!

"Watch where you're going, Polly," teased James. "Hold your head up!"

That night, Polly was too excited to sleep. She stayed up late and wrote in her diary:

Dear Diary,
        Tomorrow is the wedding!

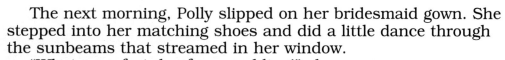

The next morning, Polly slipped on her bridesmaid gown. She stepped into her matching shoes and did a little dance through the sunbeams that streamed in her window.

"What a perfect day for a wedding!" she sang.

James wasn't allowed to see the bride before the wedding, but Polly couldn't resist taking a peek.

Rebecca looked gorgeous in her new bridal gown! She borrowed her mother's pearls and wore the same veil her grandmother wore when she got married.

"These are the things brides wear for luck," she told Polly.

"Something old, something new,
Something borrowed, something blue."

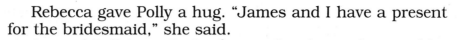

Rebecca gave Polly a hug. "James and I have a present for the bridesmaid," she said.

Around Polly's neck she fastened a shiny silver necklace with a pretty heart in the middle.

"Oh, thank you!" exclaimed Polly. "I love it!"

11

Ding-ding dong! Ding-ding dong! The bells were ringing merrily as Polly arrived at the wedding chapel. It was nearly time for the ceremony to begin.

But as she hurried along the walkway toward the side entrance, James burst through the door looking terribly upset. "I've lost the rings!" he cried.

Oh no, thought Polly. James and Rebecca can't get married without wedding rings.

"Don't worry, James," she said calmly, pulling two satin ribbons from her bouquet. "I'll make you some rings."

Quickly Polly looped the ribbons around a clean, dry twig. She tied neat knots, then carefully slid the ribbon rings off the stick.

"Thank you, Polly," James said. "They're beautiful."

"They'll have to do," replied Polly. "But I hope Rebecca isn't too surprised during the ceremony!"

Polly stood in the rear of the wedding chapel. The organ music started. Suddenly the aisle looked very long, and Polly felt butterflies in her stomach.

But James turned and gave her a wink and a mischievous grin. Polly smiled back, held up her head, and walked slowly down the aisle.

Then the music changed, and everyone stood up. Here comes the bride, thought Polly, quivering with excitement.

Rebecca looked lovelier than ever. Her eyes sparkled as she glided down the aisle on the arm of her father.

Polly saw that James couldn't take his eyes off his bride. And she saw Rebecca's mother wipe away a few happy tears. I'll always remember this moment, Polly told herself.

Rebecca and James stood side by side, and the ceremony began. Polly listened carefully. She didn't want to miss one word.

Then Rebecca handed Polly her bouquet, and James took the ribbon rings from his pocket.

Rebecca's eyes widened in surprise when she saw the pink, satin ring that James slipped onto her finger. James leaned over and whispered something into her ear, and Rebecca nodded. She took the blue ring and put it on James's finger.

19

Rebecca looked into James's eyes and smiled. The happy couple kissed, and the ceremony was complete.

Rebecca and James were married! Hand in hand they ran down the steps of the chapel. Everyone threw rice at them for good luck.

The wedding reception was held on the lawn. Sunlight sparkled on the pretty goldfish pond, and the gazebo was trimmed with flowering vines and lacy bows. Polly had never seen such splendid decorations!

Polly wondered if Rebecca felt disappointed at not having her gold wedding ring. But Rebecca was laughing and talking with all the guests. She seemed to be having a marvelous time.

There were toasts and songs, music and dancing, lots of gifts, and a fancy wedding cake with a tiny bride and groom on top.

Polly had so much fun that she wished the day could go on and on. But soon Rebecca and James slipped away from the celebration to change before leaving on their honeymoon.

Rebecca threw her bridal bouquet high into the air and all the girls ran to catch it. The bouquet flew right into Polly's hands!

"I guess you're the next to marry," Rebecca laughed.

Everyone clapped, and Polly felt herself blushing. She looked down shyly. Then something shiny in the pond caught her eye.

Polly walked along the mossy bank and peered into the water, but she couldn't see anything shiny. It was probably just one of the goldfish, she told herself.

Then suddenly she stopped. "Rebecca! James!" Polly called. "Come quickly!" She kneeled, reached into the water, and scooped up two gold rings!

"Polly, you're a wonder!" declared James when he saw what she had found. "I walked here by the pond before the wedding, and the rings must have fallen out then."

Rebecca and James were very glad to have their gold rings back. "But I'll always keep the one you made, Polly," Rebecca told her. "Thanks to you, I have two wedding rings!"

Rebecca and James climbed into their elegant carriage. They waved and blew kisses to everyone as they drove away. "Good-bye! Good luck!" called Polly. She waved her handkerchief until they were out of sight.

As she got ready for bed that night, Polly took off the neck-lace James and Rebecca had given her. She turned the pretty heart over, and suddenly it opened.

The heart was a locket! Inside was a picture of James and Rebecca. And there was a special message for Polly.

The little bridesmaid smiled and lay back on her pillow. She closed her eyes, and before long she was dreaming happy dreams of her own wedding day.